TIMELINES OF
AMERICAN HISTORY ™

A Timeline of the Supreme Court

Mick Isle

rosen central ™

The Rosen Publishing Group, Inc., New York

To squiddles at 32 and Skippy Food Fair

Published in 2004 by The Rosen Publishing Group, Inc.
29 East 21st Street, New York, NY 10010

First Edition

Library of Congress Cataloging-in-Publication Data

Isle, Mick, 1966–
A timeline of the Supreme Court / Mick Isle.— 1st ed.
    p. cm. — (Timelines of American history)
Summary: Provides a chronological look at the history of the United States Supreme Court, the judges who have made their mark there, and the cases which have been important in each century.
Includes bibliographical references and index.
ISBN 0-8239-4541-3 (library binding)
1. United States. Supreme Court—History—Juvenile literature. [1. United States. Supreme Court—History. 2. Judges.] I. Title. II. Series.
KF8742.Z9S67 2004
347.73'26'09—dc22

                                                              2003016106

Manufactured in the United States of America

On the cover: Chief Justice Chase at a Supreme Court hearing in 1867.
On the title page: The chief justices of the United States, Chicago, May 4, 1894

Contents

1 The Supreme Court   **4**

2 The Nineteenth Century   **8**

3 The Early Twentieth Century   **14**

4 The Later Twentieth Century   **18**

What Is a Timeline?   **28**

Glossary   **29**

Web Sites   **30**

Index   **31**

1

The Supreme Court

When the Founding Fathers sat down to write the U.S. Constitution, they created a safety system of checks and balances. Under this system, the government would be made up of three parts, or branches: executive (the president), legislative (Congress), and judicial (the Supreme Court). Each branch had an equal share of power. No branch could make decisions without the approval of the other two branches. In the beginning, however, the Supreme Court's role wasn't very clear. This resulted in the Court having less power than the president and Congress.

The Founding Fathers signed the United States Constitution in Independence Hall, Philadelphia, in 1787. Out of fifty-five delegates at the Constitutional Convention, only thirty-nine signed the Constitution. They ranged in age from twenty-six to eighty-one.

★ 1775

The beginning of the American Revolution. American troops fight for independence from the British king who rules the thirteen American colonies.

★ 1787

Now that the United States is an independent nation, the Founding Fathers meet in Philadelphia to write the Constitution. The Constitution is a list of guidelines on how the new country will be governed. Article III discusses the creation of the U.S. Supreme Court but says nothing about its specific responsibilities.

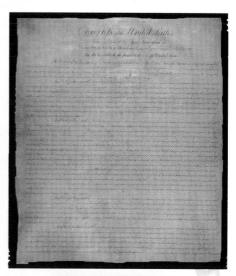

Judiciary Act of 1789

★ 1789

The first law to be introduced in the United States Senate is the Judiciary Act of 1789. This law gives the president the power to nominate the Supreme Court's justices. The Court is to meet, or "sit," in the nation's capital.

★ February 2, 1789

The Supreme Court meets for the first time. The chief justice is John Jay (born in New York City in 1745). The Court's first job is to decide what its duties will be.

Chief Justices

Sixteen chief justices have presided over the U.S. Supreme Court since it was created. Chief justices are chosen by the president. Many chief justices influenced the Court and the American justice system. During his thirty-four years as chief justice, John Marshall turned the Court into the highest court in the land. This meant that when the Supreme Court made a decision, it was final. Nobody could argue with the Court because its decision was considered the last word.

An 1852 image of the Merchants' Exchange, the first location of the Supreme Court. Located between Wall Street and Exchange Place in New York City, the Court was in the heart of the business center of Manhattan.

1790
The Supreme Court's first home is in the Merchants' Exchange Building in New York City, the nation's first capital. Later in the year, the U.S. capital moves to Philadelphia and the Court goes, too, first to Independence Hall, then to City Hall.

1792
The Supreme Court hears its first case.

August 12, 1795
President George Washington nominates John Rutledge as chief justice. Rutledge was born in Charleston, South Carolina, in September 1739.

President George Washington

March 3, 1796
President George Washington nominates Oliver Ellsworth for the position of chief justice. Ellsworth was born on April 29, 1745, in Windsor, Connecticut.

1800
Washington, D.C., becomes the permanent capital of the United States. Since it has no building of its own, Congress lends the Court various meeting rooms in the new Capitol.

1801
Supreme Court justices begin the tradition of wearing black robes in the Court.

2

The Nineteenth Century

Chief Justice John Marshall outlined the role of the Supreme Court and the entire United States judiciary (legal) system. He began with the landmark case *Marbury v. Madison.* This case defined the idea of "constitutionality." When justices look at the constitutionality of an act or law, they try to decide whether it agrees with or goes against amendments set down in the United States Constitution. For the justices, the Constitution is the supreme law of the land and guides all of their decisions.

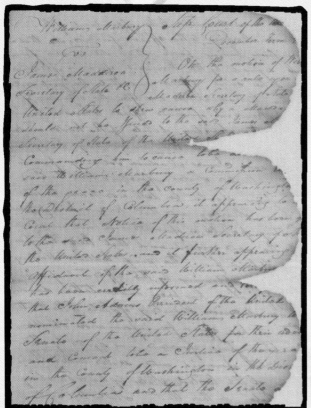

This document, part of the *Marbury v. Madison* decision, was written by Chief Justice John Marshall. It was damaged in a fire at the Capitol in 1898, which is why some of the writing is missing.

⭐ 1800

President John Adams appoints John Marshall as the fourth chief justice of the Supreme Court. Marshall was born on September 24, 1755, in Germantown, Virginia. Under the strong leadership of Marshall, the Supreme Court fought for its equal share of power laid out in the Constitution's system of checks and balances.

⭐ 1803

In *Marbury v. Madison*, the Court makes itself the highest authority of justice in the country. From now on, only the Supreme Court has the power to interpret the words and meaning of the Constitution.

⭐ 1812

At age thirty-three, Joseph Story becomes the youngest associate justice. Story was born in Marblehead, Massachusetts, in 1779.

Chief Justice John Marshall

⭐ 1819

In *McCulloch v. Maryland*, the Court decides that a federal government law is stronger than a state government law.

⭐ 1824

In *Gibbons v. Ogden*, the Court decides that the federal government can control all types of trade between the states.

Important Cases of the Nineteenth Century

During the 1800s, many of the Supreme Court's major decisions dealt with conflicts between the federal (national) and state governments. In general, the Court ruled that federal laws had more authority, or power, than state laws. Meanwhile, in terms of race relations, the

Court's decisions increased racism against blacks by supporting the legal separation of blacks and whites. Although slavery was made illegal in 1865, the famous case *Dred Scott v. Sanford* was a setback to blacks seeking equal rights as American citizens. Years of discrimination against blacks wouldn't be corrected until the civil rights era of the twentieth century.

This is the front page of *Frank Leslie's Illustrated Newspaper*, which covered the Dred Scott case. The newspaper, which ran from 1855 to 1922, was the first successful weekly newspaper in America that combined pictures and news. Frank Leslie lived from 1821 to 1880.

1835

John Marshall dies. President Andrew Jackson appoints Roger Brooke Taney as the Court's fifth chief justice. Taney was born in Calvert County, Maryland, on March 17, 1777.

1857

In *Dred Scott v. Sanford*, the Court rules that, under the United States Constitution, blacks are not citizens.

1861

The American Civil War begins. Confederate troops from the South battle Union troops from the North.

1864

Salmon Portland Chase becomes chief justice. Chase was born in Cornish, New Hampshire, on January 13, 1808. He was raised in Ohio.

1865

The Civil War ends. The South surrenders to the North. President Abraham Lincoln approves the Thirteenth Amendment to the Constitution, which ends slavery in the United States.

1869

The number of Supreme Court justices is permanently set at nine.

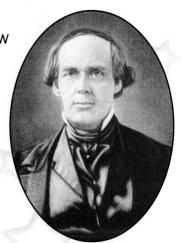

Chief Justice
Salmon Portland Chase

Life at the Supreme Court

During more than 200 years of history, the Supreme Court has kept up many traditions. Justices sit in the same black robes and write with the same white quills that were used in the Court's earliest days. Although they might not be scolded or sent away as they were in the past, lawyers are still expected to arrive in court dressed in "formal" clothes.

Meanwhile, the Court continued to support racism between black and white Americans when it made its famous "separate but equal" ruling in the case *Plessy v. Ferguson*.

From left to right, Justice Bradley, Justice Blatchford, Justice Miller, Justice Mathews, Chief Justice Waite, Justice Grey, Justice Field, Justice Lamar, and Justice Harlan. This portrait of the Supreme Court justices was taken in 1888.

1874

Morrison R. Waite becomes chief justice. Waite was born on November 29, 1816, in Lyme, Connecticut.

1888

Melville W. Fuller becomes chief justice and creates the conference hand-shake. When meeting each day, the first thing justices do is shake hands with each other. This is to remind them that although they may disagree, they must deliver justice as one agreeable group.

Chief Justice
Melville W. Fuller

1890

"Who is that beast who dares come before us in a gray coat?" says Associate Justice Horace Gray when a young lawyer comes to Court dressed in "street clothes."

1896

In *Plessy v. Ferguson*, the Court rules that having "separate" facilities—such as schools, seating in theaters and bathrooms—for blacks and whites is constitutional as long as the facilities are "equal."

3

The Early Twentieth Century

The Supreme Court is made up of one chief justice and eight associate justices. They hold their jobs for life—until they retire or die. Since its creation, ninety-seven associate justices have served on the Court. Only two have been women.

In Austin, Texas, on Monday, January 6, 2003, U.S. Supreme Court Justice Sandra Day O'Connor gives the oath of office to Justice Schneider (left), Chief Justice Phillips, and Justice Jefferson (right).

In general, presidents select justices who share their political views. Because of this, the Court's interpretations of the Constitution tend to change over time. Depending on its justices—and who appointed them—the Court's decisions may have more in common with Democratic or Republican ways of thinking.

★ **1909**
At age sixty-five, Horace Lurton, is the oldest associate justice to be elected to serve on the Supreme Court. He was born in Kentucky on February 26, 1844.

Lurton was nominated by President William H. Taft, who was a Democrat.

1910
Edward D. White becomes chief justice. He was born in Lafourche Parish, Louisiana, on November 3, 1845.

1916
Louis Brandeis (born in 1856 in Louisville, Kentucky) becomes the first Jewish associate justice to serve on the Supreme Court. Many people were against Brandeis becoming a justice because of his religion. In fact, another associate justice refused to sit beside him during meetings of the Court.

Louis Brandeis was very concerned with individual rights and freedom of speech. Before President Woodrow Wilson nominated Brandeis for his position at the Supreme Court, Brandeis had been a very successful lawyer. He died in Washington, D.C., in 1941.

Chief Justice William H. Taft

1921
Former president William H. Taft becomes chief justice. Taft was born in Cincinnati, Ohio, on September 15, 1857.

15

The Building

The Supreme Court spent its first 146 years without its own building. The architect Cass Gilbert was selected to design a building "of dignity and importance." The Supreme Court is a four-story marble building. It copied many elements of the architecture of

ancient Rome, such as marble columns and a grand central staircase. The $9.7 million spent on the building covered construction costs, decoration, and furniture. There was even money left over to return to the U.S. Treasury!

This is a view of the 252-foot-wide (76.8-meter-wide) oval plaza and the United States Supreme Court Building in Washington, D.C. On both sides of the plaza are fountains, benches, and flagpoles. The building can be visited during the week.

1929
Chief Justice William Howard Taft persuades Congress to construct a permanent home for the Supreme Court. The architect Cass Gilbert is chosen to design the new building. A few years earlier, Gilbert had also designed the Woolworth Building, one of New York City's first skyscrapers.

Architect Cass Gilbert

1930
Charles E. Hughes becomes chief justice. He was born in Glens Falls, New York, on April 11, 1862.

1932
Construction of the new Supreme Court Building begins. On January 12, ninety-year-old Oliver Wendell Holmes Jr. is the oldest justice to retire from the Supreme Court.

1935
The Court finally moves into its new home at First Street Northeast and East Capitol Street, in Washington, D.C.

1941
Harlan F. Stone becomes chief justice. Stone was born on October 11, 1872, in Chesterfield, New Hampshire.

1945
The Supreme Court handles 1,460 cases.

1946
Frederick M. Vinson becomes chief justice. He was born in Louisa, Kentucky, on January 22, 1890.

17

4

The Later Twentieth Century

In America, the 1950s and 1960s are known as the civil rights era. "Minorities"—women and people of different races and different religions—fought to be treated like the "majority" of white male Christian citizens. To give minorities greater chances at equality, many schools and businesses adopted programs with quota systems. Quotas, or limits, guaranteed a set number of places to minorities who, in the past, had suffered from discrimination.

Over the years, the Supreme Court has struggled to support civil rights without creating what some view as "reverse discrimination" against white males.

The official seal of the United States Supreme Court

1953

In October, Earl Warren is named chief justice. He is appointed by President Dwight D. Eisenhower. For the sixteen years that Warren is chief justice, the Court is known as the "Warren court," because many of its decisions reflect his views.

On the steps of the Supreme Court, Nettie Hunt explains the meaning of the *Brown v. Board of Education* case to her daughter, Nickie. The photo was taken in May 1954.

Warren becomes chief justice at the beginning of the civil rights movement, during which Americans are demanding equal rights for all. During this time, the Court makes many important decisions that help minorities gain the same rights as other citizens.

1954

In *Brown v. Board of Education*, the Court overturns the 1896 "separate but equal" ruling that it made in *Plessy v. Ferguson*. It rules that having "separate" schools for blacks and whites is "unequal."

1961

The Supreme Court handles 2,313 cases.

Justice for All

The Warren court made many important rulings that challenged traditional ideas and institutions. In the 1950s and 1960s, fighting for civil rights included battling for equal rights to justice under American law. Since the 1960s, an important role of the Supreme Court has been to make sure that all Americans can seek justice, no matter who

they are or where they live. The Court has also supported one of the most important elements of American law: it states that all suspects are considered innocent until proven guilty.

A portrait of Thurgood Marshall. Marshall was nominated to the United States Supreme Court in 1967. He served there until his retirement in June 1991. Before serving on the Supreme Court, Marshall served as legal director of the NAACP (National Association for the Advancement of Colored People).

1961

In *Mapp v. Ohio*, the Court rules that evidence found by "lawless [illegal] means [methods]" cannot be used in a court of law.

1962

In *Engel v. Vitale*, the Court rules that prayer is not allowed in school, supporting the Constitution's separation of church and state.

1963

In *Gideon v. Wainwright*, the Court rules that if a defendant (someone charged with a crime) has no money for a lawyer, a court must select one for him or her.

1966

In *Miranda v. Arizona*, the Court rules that law officials must inform suspects of their legal rights before questioning them.

An original Miranda rights card

1967

Thurgood Marshall becomes the first black associate justice. He was born in Baltimore, Maryland, in 1908.

1969

Warren E. Burger becomes chief justice. He was born in 1907 in St. Paul, Minnesota.

Life and Death

One of the most argued-over issues in the United States is the death penalty. In some states, criminals found guilty of serious crimes, such as murder, can be put to death. The Eighth Amendment of the United States Constitution says "cruel and unusual punishment shall not be inflicted [applied]" to citizens who have committed a crime. Over the last thirty years, the Supreme Court has had to make difficult decisions concerning the death penalty.

On June 30, 1992, abortion activists—both pro (for) and con (against)—face each other outside the Supreme Court Building. The Court had ruled to uphold Pennsylvania's restrictive abortion laws.

1972

In *Furman v. Georgia*, for the first time ever, the Court rules against the death penalty. The Court argues that it goes against the Eighth Amendment.

1973

In *Roe v. Wade*, the Court makes illegal any law that prevents a woman from having an abortion during the first three months of pregnancy.

1976

In *Gregg v. Georgia*, the Court rules that the death penalty is constitutional. It is legal as long as juries know that they can choose between death and other forms of punishment such as life in prison.

Sandra Day O'Connor

1980

William O. Douglas retires, having spent more time in office than any other justice (36 years and 209 days). Douglas was born on October 16, 1898, in Maine, Minnesota.

1981

Sandra Day O'Connor becomes the first female associate justice. She was born in 1930 in El Paso, Texas.

Freedom of Speech

Most Americans see freedom of speech as the most basic of rights. Freedom of speech means being able to say or write or express yourself in public, no matter what your opinion is. Free speech is guaranteed by the First Amendment of the Constitution. Yet, in the last thirty years, the Supreme Court has been asked to decide more cases about freedom of speech than in the first 175 years of

United States Supreme Court justice William H. Rehnquist gives a lecture at the University of Virginia School of Law in Charlottesville, Virginia, on April 11, 2003.

its existence. Free speech is not limited to the spoken and written word. Wearing a T-shirt with a printed peace symbol or burning a flag can also be considered forms of expression.

★ **1986**
William H. Rehnquist becomes chief justice. He was born in 1934 in Milwaukee, Wisconsin.

★ **1988**
In *Hustler Magazine v. Falwell*, the Court supports freedom of speech when it says that *Hustler* has a right to criticize or make fun of a public figure.

★ **1988**
In *Hazelwood School District v. Kuhlmeier*, the Court rules that school officials can control what is written in a student newspaper. The decision limits students' freedom of speech.

★ **1989**
In *Texas v. Johnson*, the Court extends the meaning of freedom of speech when it supports a man's right to burn the American flag as a sign of protest.

Protestors burn the American flag on June 14, 1990.

Court Procedure

The Supreme Court meets between October and June. This period is called a term. Each term is made up of sittings and recesses. During sittings, judges listen to cases. During recesses, they discuss and then write out decisions. All nine judges rarely reach the same decision. Often, opinions are split between the majority (five or more justices

This drawing, by court artist Franklin McMahon, shows what was going on inside the Supreme Court Building during the famous case of President Richard Nixon, which took place in 1974.

whose opinions become the final ruling) and the minority, or dissenters (the four or fewer justices who disagree with the majority).

As society changes, new questions come up. In the last ten years, the Court has been faced with new and complicated cases ranging from gay rights to a patient's right to die.

★ **1990**

In *Cruzan v. Missouri Department of Health*, the Court rules that a dying patient capable of making a decision can refuse medical treatment to keep him or her alive.

★ **1996**

In *Romer v. Evans*, the Court supports gay and lesbian rights, arguing that the Constitution protects the rights of all American citizens.

★ **1997**

In *Printz v. United States*, the Court says the federal government can't force state governments to follow federal gun control laws if they have their own gun laws.

★ **2000**

Of the 7,000 cases that come before the Supreme Court, only about 250 cases are heard.

What Is a Timeline?

Timelines can be very helpful for people studying history. They provide an outline of important events organized according to the years in which they happened. Events are ordered from the earliest to the most recent. In one look, you can easily see what happened and when. You can also discover how one event can lead to another over a long period of time. Timelines are a great beginning. They give you basic facts and dates that serve as useful guides when you need to research individual subjects in depth.

Glossary

abortion (uh-BOR-shun) The termination of a pregnancy.

appoint (uh-POYNT) To officially name or choose someone for a job.

civil rights (SIH-vul RYTS) Rights of personal freedom to be equally shared by all American citizens under the U.S. Constitution.

Civil War (SIH-vul WOR) The war fought between the Northern and Southern states of America between 1861 and 1865.

constitution (kon-stih-TOO-shun) A country's written system of rules that outlines the powers and duties of the government and protects citizens' rights.

discrimination (dih-skrih-mih-NAY-shun) Treating a person badly or unfairly just because he or she is different.

dissenter (dih-SEN-ter) Someone who doesn't agree with a popular opinion.

facilities (fuh-SI-li-teez) Something built to provide a particular service (such as a cafeteria, health clinic, or restroom).

interpret (in-TER-priht) To explain or tell the meaning of something (for example, a document, book, or poem).

justice (JUS-tis) A judge.

landmark case (LAND-MARK KAYS) A case that marks a turning point or leads to an important change.

nominate (NAH-mih-nayt) To suggest that someone or something should be given an award or a position.

preside (prih-ZYD) To guide or direct.

quill (KWIL) A pen made from a feather.

quota (KWO-tah) A share or portion given to each member of a group.

recess (REE-ses) A pause or rest from one's normal work routine.

Web Sites

Due to the changing nature of Internet links, the Rosen Publishing Group, Inc., has developed on online list of Web sites related to the subject of this book. This site is updated regularly. Please use this link to access the list:

http://www.rosenlinks.com/tah/suco

Index

A

Adams, John, 9

B

Brandeis, Louis, 15
Brown v. Board of Education, 19
Burger, Warren E., 21

C

Chase, Salmon Portland, 11
civil rights, 10, 18, 19, 20, 27
Civil War, 11
Congress, 4, 7, 17
Constitution, U.S., 4, 5, 8, 9, 11, 14, 21, 22, 24
Cruzan v. Missouri Department of Health, 27

D

death penalty, 22, 23
Douglas, William O., 23
Dred Scott v. Sanford, 10, 11

E

Eisenhower, Dwight D., 19
Ellsworth, Oliver, 7
Engel v. Vitale, 21

F

federal government, 4, 9, 10, 27
Founding Fathers, 4, 5
freedom of speech, 24–25
Fuller, Melville W., 13
Furman v. Georgia, 23

G

Gibbons v. Ogden, 9
Gideon v. Wainwright, 21
Gilbert, Cass, 16, 17
Gray, Horace, 13
Gregg v. Georgia, 23

H

Hazelwood School District v. Kuhlmeier, 25
Holmes, Oliver Wendell, Jr., 17
Hughes, Charles E., 17
Hustler Magazine v. Falwell, 25

J

Jackson, Andrew, 11
Jay, John, 5

L

lawyers, 12, 13
Lincoln, Abraham, 11
Lurton, Horace, 14

M

Mapp v. Ohio, 21
Marbury v. Madison, 8, 9
Marshall, John, 6, 8, 9, 11
Marshall, Thurgood, 21
McCulloch v. Maryland, 9
minorities, 18, 19
Miranda v. Arizona, 21

N

New York City, 5, 7, 17

O

O'Connor, Sandra Day, 23

P

Philadelphia, 5, 7
Plessy v. Ferguson, 12, 13, 19
president, 4, 5, 6, 7, 14
Printz v. United States, 27

R

racism/discrimination, 10, 11, 12, 13, 18
Rehnquist, William H., 25
Roe v. Wade, 23
Romer v. Evans, 27
Rutledge, John, 7

S

"separate but equal," 12, 13, 19

A Timeline of the Supreme Court

slavery, 10, 11
state governments, 9,
    10, 27
Stone, Harlan F., 17
Story, Joseph, 9
Supreme Court
  and civil rights, 18, 19
  creation of, 4, 5
  in early twentieth century,
    14–17
  in late twentieth century,
    18–27

locations of, 7, 17
in nineteenth century, 8–13
number of justices, 11, 14
powers/role of, 4, 5, 6, 8,
    9, 20
procedures of, 26–27
traditions of, 7, 12, 13
Supreme Court Building,
    16, 17

T

Taft, William H., 15, 17

Taney, Roger Brooke, 11
Texas v. Johnson, 25

V

Vinson, Frederick M., 17

W

Waite, Morrison R., 13
Warren, Earl, 19, 20
Washington, D.C., 7, 17
Washington, George, 7
White, Edward D., 15

Credits

About the author: Mick Isle is a freelance journalist.

Photo credits: cover © North Wind Pictures; pp. 1, 10, 11, 12, 15 (bottom), 19 ©
Library of Congress Print and Photographs Division; pp. 4, 13 © Hulton Archive/Getty
Images; p. 5 © General Records of the United States government, National Archives and
Records Administration; p. 6 © Archivo Iconografico, S.A./Corbis; pp. 7, 20 © Corbis;
p. 8 © Records of the Supreme Court of the United States, National Archives and
Records Administration; pp. 9, 15 (top), 17, 18, 21 © Bettmann/Corbis; pp. 14, 22, 24
© AP/World Wide Photos; p. 16 © Owen Franken/Corbis; p. 23 © Reuters NewMedia
Inc./Corbis; p. 25 © Jacques M. Chenet/Corbis; p. 26 © Franklin McMahon/Corbis.

Designer: Geri Fletcher; Editor: Annie Sommers